A Book of Sleep

Il Sung Na

ALFRED A. KNOPF
NEW YORK

When the sky grows dark
and the moon glows bright,
everyone goes to sleep…

R0423415082

...except for the watchful owl.

Some sleep
in peace and quiet.

Some make lots of noise
when they sleep.

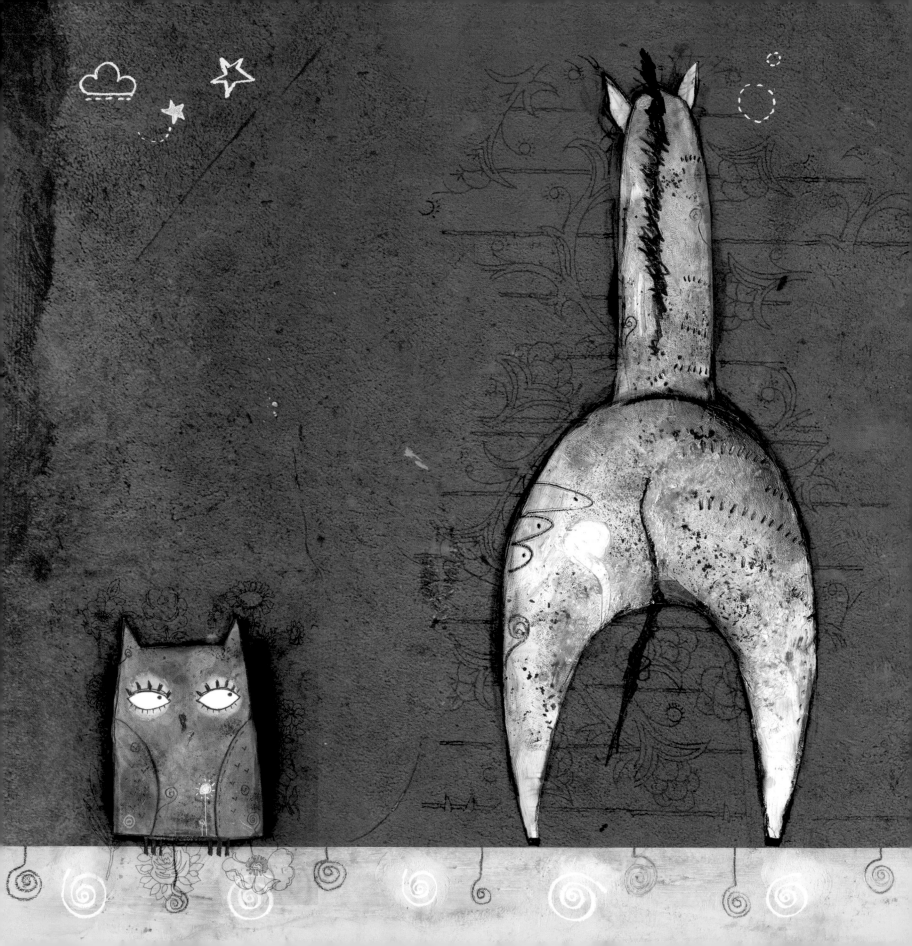

Some sleep standing up,

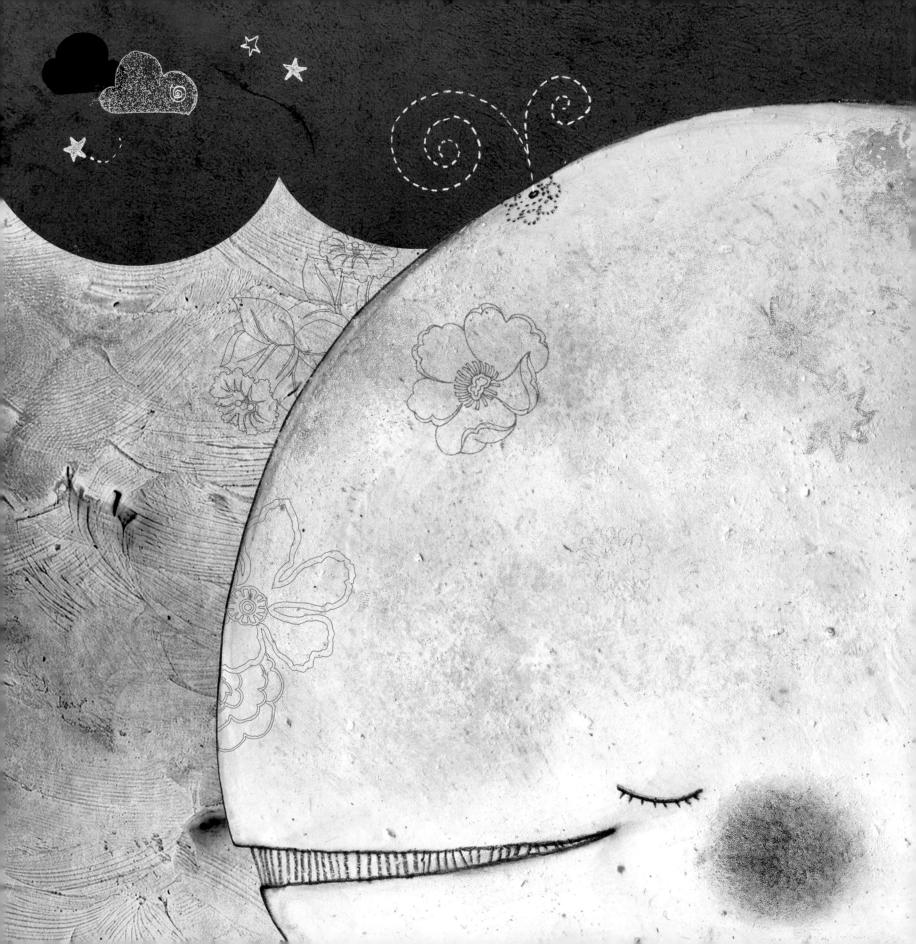

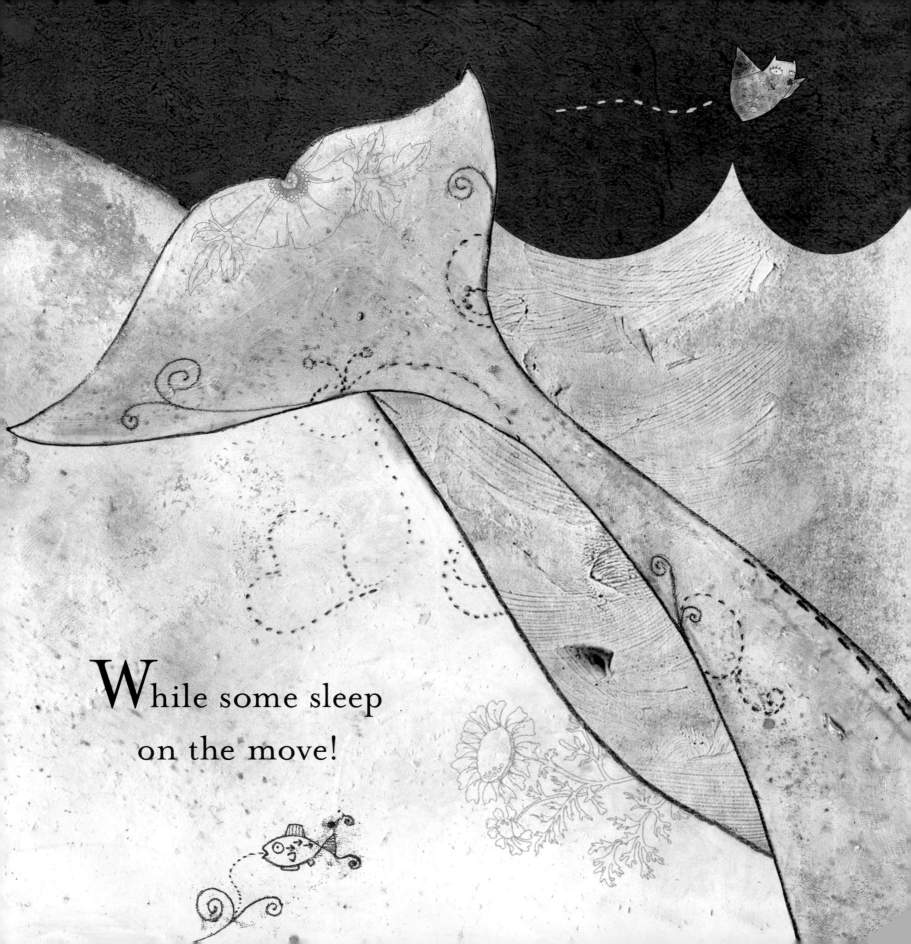

While some sleep
on the move!

Some sleep with
one eye open.

Some sleep with *both* eyes open...

Some sleep peacefully alone,

While others sleep all together,
huddled close at night.

But when the sky turns
blue and the sun
glows bright…

…everyone wakes up!

Except for the tired owl.

zzz

For Mum and Dad

THIS IS A BORZOI BOOK PUBLISHED BY ALFRED A. KNOPF

Copyright © 2007 by Il Sung Na

All rights reserved. Published in the United States by Alfred A. Knopf, an imprint of Random House Children's Books,
a division of Random House, Inc., New York. Originally published in slightly different form in Great Britain as
Zzzz: A Book of Sleep by Meadowside Children's Books, London, in 2007.

Knopf, Borzoi Books, and the colophon are registered trademarks of Random House, Inc.

Visit us on the Web! www.randomhouse.com/kids

Educators and librarians, for a variety of teaching tools, visit us at
www.randomhouse.com/teachers

Library of Congress Cataloging-in-Publication Data
Na, Il Sung.
A book of sleep / Il Sung Na. — 1st American ed.
p.   cm.
Summary: While other animals sleep at night, some quietly and others noisily,
some alone and others huddled together, a wide-eyed owl watches.
ISBN 978-0-375-86223-6 (trade) — ISBN 978-0-375-96223-3 (lib. bdg.)
[1. Owls—Juvenile fiction. 2. Sleep behavior in animals—Juvenile fiction. 3. Owls—Fiction.
4. Animals—Sleep behavior—Fiction.] I. Title.
PZ10.3.N12Boo 2009
[E]—dc22
2008047865

The illustrations in this book were created by combining handmade painterly textures with
digitally generated layers, which were then compiled in Adobe Photoshop.

MANUFACTURED IN CHINA
September 2009
10 9 8 7 6 5 4 3 2 1
First American Edition

Random House Children's Books supports the First Amendment and celebrates the right to read.